84-18

636.9
MEY   Meyers, Susan

                Pearson, a harbor
                seal pup

DATE DUE

PEARSON
A Harbor Seal Pup

PEARSON
A Harbor Seal Pup

written by Susan Meyers

photographed by Ilka Hartmann

E. P. DUTTON   NEW YORK

For my mother . . . with love and appreciation.
S.M.

For my son Ole, who had the great fortune
to spend part of his early life
near one of his brothers from the sea.
I.H.

Text copyright © 1980 by Susan Meyers
Photographs copyright © 1980 by Ilka Hartmann

Library of Congress Cataloging in Publication Data

Meyers, Susan.   Pearson, a harbor seal pup.

Summary: Describes the growth and development of an
orphaned harbor seal pup from his arrival at the California
Marine Mammal Center to the time of his release into the ocean.
1. Harbor seal—Juvenile literature.   2. Wildlife rescue—
Juvenile literature.   [1. Harbor seal.   2. Seals (Animals)
3. Wildlife rescue.]   I. Hartmann, Ilka.   II. Title.
QL737.P64M49   1980   636'.9748   80-13041
ISBN: 0-525-36845-0

Published in the United States by E. P. Dutton, a Division
of Elsevier-Dutton Publishing Company, Inc., New York

Published simultaneously in Canada by Clarke,
Irwin & Company Limited, Toronto and Vancouver

Editor: Ann Troy   Designer: Stacie Rogoff

Printed in the U.S.A.   First Edition
10 9 8 7 6 5 4 3 2

ACKNOWLEDGMENTS

This book could never have been completed without the kind and generous cooperation of the staff and volunteers at the California Marine Mammal Center. All were consistently patient and helpful, giving of their time as well as their knowledge.

Special thanks must go to Bill Keener, Bob Wilson, Margie Pharis, Mary Gilman, Chris Hempel, Anne Kania, Anne Woessner, and Lloyd Smalley.

Last—but very far from least—we are indebted to Holly Garner, who entered into the spirit of the project with enthusiasm and who, more than anyone else, was responsible for the successful rehabilitation and release of Pearson, the harbor seal pup.

The pup was an orphan. He was found one morning in April, alone and half-starved, on a deserted beach in northern California. Like all young harbor seals, he had soft, gray-spotted fur and big, dark eyes. He moved by inching along the sand on his belly, and he made a plaintive *krooh, krooh* sound like the mooing of a hungry calf.

No one knew what had happened to his mother. The woman who found him watched and waited to see if the mother seal would return. But she didn't. Perhaps she was dead. She may have been killed by a shark or a hunter. Without someone to feed and protect him, the pup would die.

So the woman made a phone call. She called the California Marine Mammal Center. And that afternoon, the seal's new life began.

The Marine Mammal Center is located on the coast of the Pacific Ocean, just outside the city of San Francisco. It is a combination hospital, orphanage, and shelter for sick and abandoned seals and sea lions. Most of the people who work there are volunteers who have a special interest in marine mammals. They give the animals brought to the Center the medical attention they need. They feed and care for them until they are healthy enough to be returned to the sea.

On the afternoon in April when the orphaned pup arrived, nine elephant seals and three harbor seal pups were already at the Center. Holly Garner, the acting curator, greeted the new seal. She stroked his sleek body and let him sniff her hand with his whiskered nose.

The pup was thin, but his eyes were bright and alert. He was no more than two weeks old. In his short life, all he had known was the sea and the sand and the comfort of his mother's body. Now, human hands were holding him. But he showed no fear. He looked around curiously. He listened alertly to the strange sounds and breathed in the strange smells.

"Let's call him Pearson," Holly said. It was a good-luck name —the name of a volunteer who had worked at the Center the summer before and had had great success with harbor seal pups.

Holly hoped that this pup would be a good-luck seal. She wrote the name on a chart and then began to examine the new patient.

Caring for marine mammals—especially young ones—is not an easy task. Whales, dolphins, walruses, seals, sea lions, and sea otters are all marine mammals. Millions of years ago, their ancestors lived on land. Now, although they live in the sea, these animals breathe air, are warm-blooded, and nurse their young with milk from their bodies, just as land-living mammals do. Because they live in the oceans, however, marine mammals are difficult to study. Many things about the way they behave and the way their bodies work are not known.

The people at the Marine Mammal Center had found that harbor seal pups which were brought to them were especially difficult to raise. They were often in poor health. Usually they were very young and seriously underweight. This made them delicate and vulnerable to disease.

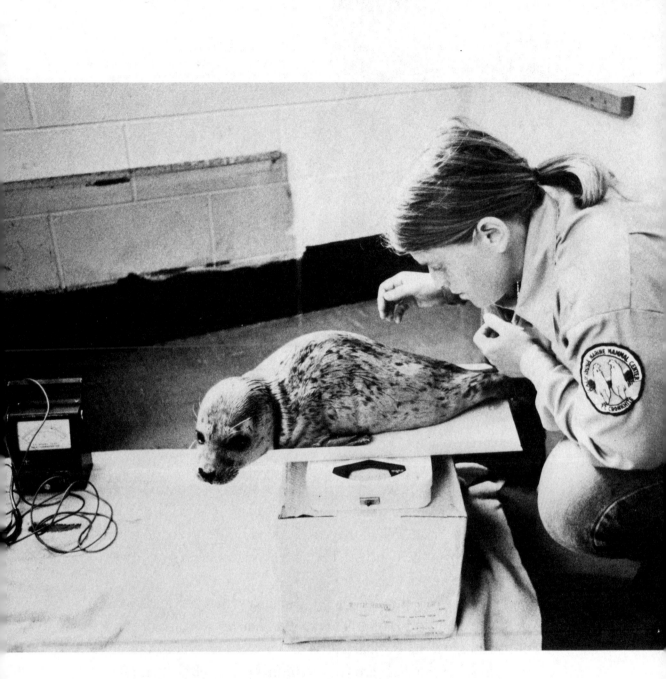

Holly was glad, then, when she put Pearson on a scale and found that he weighed 21 pounds and 2 ounces—less than a pup his age should have weighed, but still enough to give him a good start.

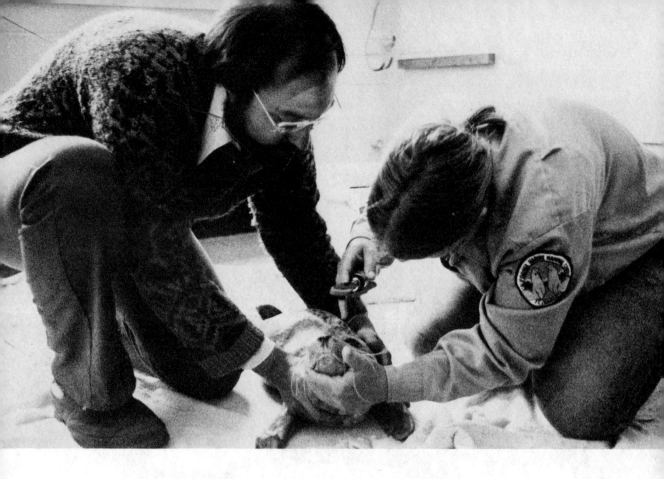

His temperature was normal. His eyes were watering. This was a good sign, too; for unlike land-living mammals, seals have no internal tear ducts. When they are in good health, tears flow continuously down their cheeks. The area beneath their eyes is always wet.

Holly opened the pup's mouth and saw that his gums were pink and healthy looking. This meant that he was not in shock or bleeding internally. Sharp little canine teeth protruded through the gums. Harbor seals are born with these teeth already in place, for they nurse only a short time and then must be able to catch fish on their own.

But that lay in the future for Pearson. Right now, he used his teeth for another purpose. As Holly took her hand away from his mouth, he reached out and nipped the sleeve of her shirt.

Holly laughed. Pearson had spunk. There was no doubt about that. He was also, as far as she could tell, in good health. She wrote the findings of her examination on his chart, and slipped it into a file folder. Then she picked him up and put him into an indoor pen with the other harbor seal pups.

Pearson scooted around the cool, cement floor of the pen. He rolled onto a blanket. He touched noses with the other pups. Then he looked up at Holly. "Krooh," he cried. It sounded almost like a question.

"Don't worry, little fellow, you're going to be okay," Holly said, as if in answer.

She hoped that she was right.

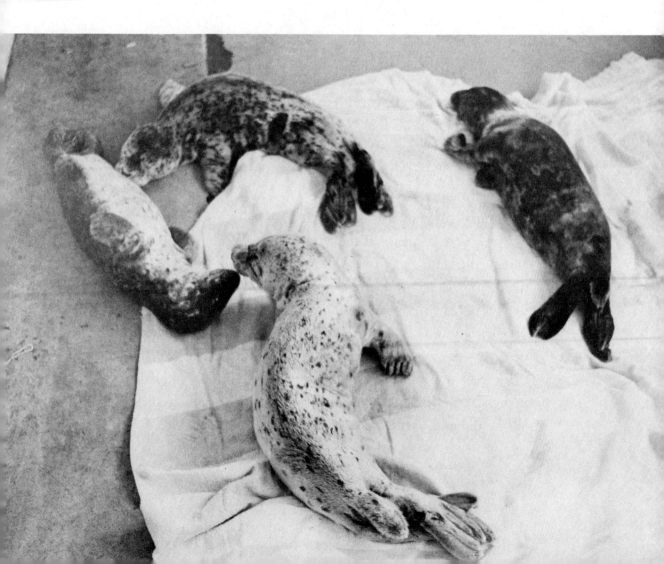

Normally, harbor seals are hardy animals. They are found in oceans and bays of the Northern Hemisphere all around the world. In the United States, they live along both the Atlantic and Pacific coasts, and are often seen swimming in harbors close to towns and cities.

Unlike marine mammals such as whales and dolphins, harbor seals do not spend all their time in the water. They hunt fish and shellfish for food, but when they are tired, they come out of the sea to rest on rocks and quiet beaches.

Their pups may be born anywhere—on a beach, in a marsh, or even in the water. The baby seal can swim—though not expertly—from the moment it takes its first breath. But in the early weeks of life, the mother seal helps it. She cradles the pup in her front flippers. She holds it close to her when she dives. When the pup is tired, she lets it ride on her back.

The pup drinks milk from its mother. This milk is about ten times richer than cow's milk. It helps the pup to grow quickly and to develop a thick layer of fat, or blubber, which protects it from the cold.

At the Marine Mammal Center, the harbor seal pups are fed a formula made from cream, butter, cod-liver oil, pureed fish, and vitamins. The formula is fed to the pups through a tube which is inserted down their throats and into their stomachs.

The first time that Pearson was fed this way, he didn't like it at all.

One volunteer had to hold him still, while another opened his mouth. Quickly and expertly, she slipped the rubber tube over his tongue and down his throat. Pearson gagged and tried to wriggle free, but the volunteer held him firmly. Slowly, the formula was poured into a funnel and down the tube.

In the past, the people who worked at the Center had tried feeding the pups from ordinary baby bottles. But this had been a failure.

A mother harbor seal has two short nipples which are buried in the fatty flesh of her underside. When she moves on her belly over rocks and sand, the nipples are protected from injury. To nurse, the pup must push its nose against her body. A nipple then moves out, and the pup grasps it between its tongue and its upper gums.

The orphaned pups didn't know what to do with a nipple which was not buried in the body of a mother seal. They couldn't seem to grasp the nipple of a baby bottle properly, and in the attempt, the rubber was quickly torn to shreds.

The only way to get the formula the pups needed into their stomachs was to feed it to them by tube.

Eventually, most of the pups got used to the tube. They didn't gag and struggle when it was inserted. In fact, some even learned to swallow the end of the tube themselves, knowing that the satisfying feeling of a full stomach would quickly follow.

When the tube was removed from Pearson's throat, he lay still with his eyes closed. It had probably been days since he had eaten. Perhaps he needed time to get used to the feeling of a full stomach again. The volunteer stroked him gently. She knew that he was now on his way to gaining back the weight he had lost while lying alone and helpless on the beach. For the first time since he had been found and brought to the Center, Pearson had a chance. With luck, he might one day grow to be a strong and healthy adult seal.

The harbor seal pups were favorites with everyone who worked at the Center, and Pearson quickly became especially popular.

He was full of energy and high spirits, and was more active than any of the other pups. When he was inside, he liked to grab the blankets spread on the floor of the pen, and drag them about with his teeth. If the gate was left open, he was always ready to slip out and have a look around.

On his diet of rich formula, he began to gain weight. Moving him from the inside pen, where the pups spent the night, to the outside pen and wading pool, where they spent the day, was a job. He was hard to hold. He had to be wrapped in a blanket so that if he wriggled, he would not slip and fall to the ground.

When Pearson had been at the Center for a week, Holly decided it was time to introduce him to fish.

In the sea, a harbor seal pup learns to catch and eat fish by watching its mother. By the time it is weaned, at the age of four or five weeks, it is able to feed on its own.

Without a mother, and living temporarily in captivity, Pearson had to be taught what a fish was and how to swallow it. Eventually, he would have to learn to catch one himself.

15

Holly started his training with a small herring—an oily fish which is a favorite with seals. Gently, she opened his mouth and slipped the fish in, headfirst. Harbor seals have sharp teeth for catching fish, but no teeth for grinding and chewing. They swallow their food whole.

But Pearson didn't seem to understand what he was supposed to do. He bit down on the fish and then spit it out. Holly tried again. This time, Pearson got the idea. He swallowed the herring in one gulp and looked eagerly for more.

Within a week, he was being hand-fed a pound of fish a day in addition to his formula. This new diet made him friskier than ever. He chased the other pups in the outside pen. He plunged into the small wading pool and rolled in the shallow water, splashing both seals and people.

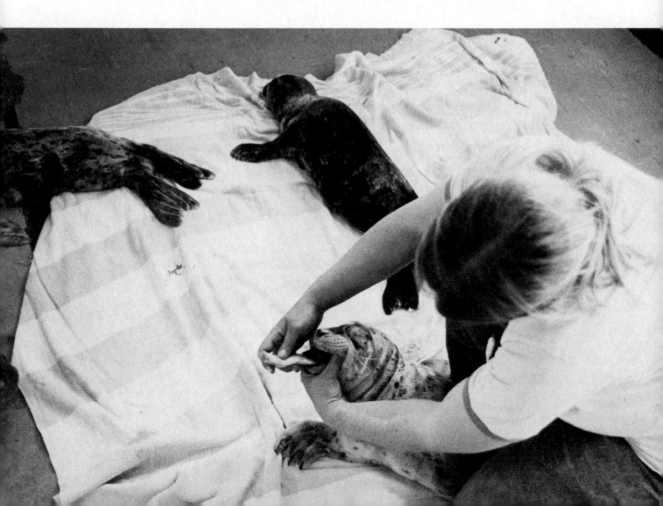

Visitors who came to the Center were eager to see the pups. Holly worried about this, for she knew that, like all young animals, the pups needed plenty of rest. There was also a possibility that a visitor might be a carrier of germs which could make a young seal sick.

One of the problems with the orphaned pups brought to the Center was that they frequently had little resistance to illness. Most young mammals gain immunity, or protection from disease, from their mother's milk. But if a pup lost its mother before it had nursed long enough, it did not have this immunity. It could easily become sick.

In addition, some of the pups had probably been born prematurely, before they had a chance to develop fully in their mothers' bodies. Others had internal birth defects. Their lungs, livers, or kidneys did not function properly. Pups like these had very likely been abandoned on purpose. The mother seals had probably sensed that something was wrong and had simply left them to die.

The people at the Marine Mammal Center did not want any of the pups to die, but sometimes there was nothing they could do to save them. One morning, the smallest harbor seal pup was found dead in the inside pen. Within a week, the other two pups who had been at the Center when Pearson arrived also sickened and died.

Everyone felt sad. They knew that in the sea, animals often die young. Among harbor seals, perhaps as many as half the pups born never reach adulthood. But still, when it happened at the Center, it was hard to take. The volunteers wondered if the right things had been done. Had they fed the pups properly? Had they watched them carefully enough? Would the pups have lived if they had tried harder?

Now Pearson was the only pup left, and suddenly he seemed more special than ever. The volunteers couldn't help regarding him anxiously. He looked healthy, but they knew that looks were no guarantee. They made up their minds to do everything within their power to keep him strong and healthy. He had had good luck so far. His human friends were determined to make it continue.

Alone in his pen, Pearson slipped into the water of the little wading pool and rolled about. But there were no other pups to splash and chase.

From time to time he cried, but mostly he was silent. Harbor seal pups make their distinctive mooing sound only when they are very young. It is a signal to the mother seal. It helps her locate her pup on the beach or in the sea. After the age of four or five weeks, when the pup no longer needs its mother, it becomes silent.

Holly felt sorry for Pearson. She decided to move him to another pen. There he would be near a pair of young elephant seals. And he would have a larger pool. It was time for some real swimming.

At first, Pearson wasn't sure what to do in his new tank. It was much bigger and deeper than the old wading pool. But soon he felt at home. As the elephant seals next door watched, he swam eagerly back and forth. Down to the bottom he dove, then up again.

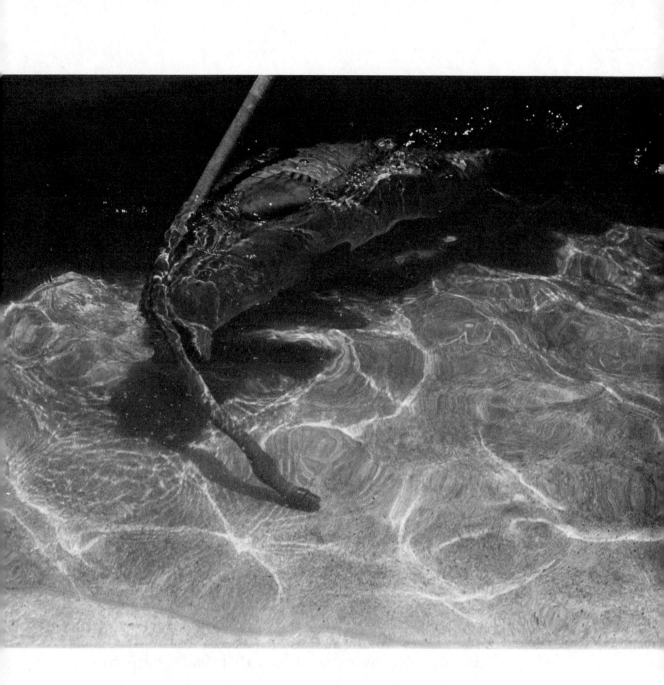

He practiced swimming on his back and on his stomach. He inspected the hose that brought fresh water into the tank. He turned in circles and chased his tail.

At mealtime, he was still swimming. Holly had to tempt him out of the pool by showing him the rubber tube that meant food. Pearson no longer had any trouble with tube feeding. Now he grabbed the end of the tube, pulled himself out of the tank, and swallowed the tube hungrily. When his feeding was over, he dozed contentedly in the late afternoon sun.

It was already May. As the warm spring days passed, Pearson grew steadily stronger. Soon he weighed 40 pounds—nearly 20 pounds more than he had weighed when he was brought to the Center.

And he had become an expert swimmer.

Like all seals, Pearson had a body which was streamlined and well suited to life in the water. When swimming, he usually kept his front flippers pressed close to his sides. He used his rear flippers as a fish uses its tail, to propel himelf quickly and gracefully forward.

He could stay underwater for five minutes or more. Adult harbor seals can remain submerged for more than twenty minutes. During this time, the seal keeps its nostrils tightly closed. Its heartbeat slows. The veins in its flippers and skin contract. Its blood—which carries oxygen—is pumped primarily to the liver, lungs, kidneys, and brain. This oxygen-rich blood keeps these vital organs healthy. They are not damaged, even though the seal is not breathing.

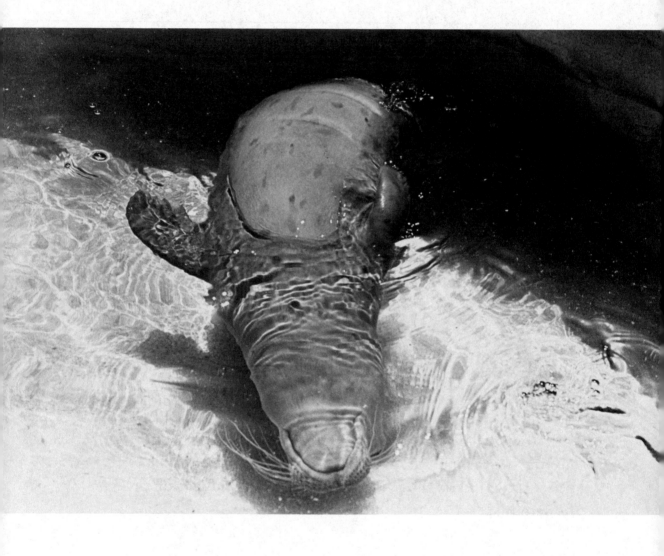

While underwater, the seal uses its keen senses to hunt for fish and to remain alert to enemies. Its eyesight and hearing are excellent. In addition, it has a special kind of sensory ability. It can detect objects underwater by a method known as echo location.

To echo locate, a seal makes clicking sounds deep in its throat. The sound waves travel through the water. When they hit an object—such as a fish—they bounce, or echo, back. The returning waves hit the seal's whiskers. These whiskers are extremely sensitive. They are connected to the seal's brain by a network of nerves. In dark waters, the seal can tell, simply by the sensations in its whiskers, exactly what an object is and where it is located.

A seal does not need to be taught to echo locate, any more than it needs to be taught to see or to hear. But it does need to learn how to catch fish once it has found them.

Pearson's hunting lessons began one morning in June.

For the past weeks, Holly and the rest of the staff had been watching the young seal closely. They had kept track of his weight and had carefully observed his appearance and behavior. As the days passed, everyone had begun to feel reassured. Pearson showed no signs of illness. His body was sleek and fat. He had developed the thick layer of blubber seals need to keep warm in the sea. He no longer needed to be fed formula or to be brought inside for the night. There seemed to be no doubt about it. Pearson was going to live.

But keeping an animal alive was only part of the struggle. Once that goal had been reached, the next job—preparing the animal for return to the sea—had to be tackled.

In the sea, Pearson's mother would have taught him all he needed to know to survive as a seal. At the Center, that job had to be taken over by his human keepers. Lessons in catching fish were the first step.

One morning, a volunteer brought Pearson's breakfast into his pen. But instead of feeding it to him by hand, as she usually did, she selected a tasty-looking herring and held it in the water in his tank. She wiggled it, making it look as if it were alive.

Pearson was curious. He swam toward the fish. He was hungry. Quickly he grabbed the herring. But instead of swallowing it at once—as he would have to do when chasing a group of fast-moving fish in the sea—he spit it out. He didn't know how to eat in this strange new way.

It took more than a week before Pearson finally learned to grab a fish in the water and swallow it at once. In another week, he was able to retrieve fish which were tossed into his tank. This made feeding time much easier. It also paved the way for the next step in Pearson's training program—learning to live without human companionship.

Harbor seals are naturally friendly and intelligent animals. In captivity, they respond affectionately to human attention. They like to be talked to and stroked. They come to know their names and to recognize the people who care for them.

The danger at the Center is that a pup like Pearson will become too attached to human beings. If he is to survive in the sea, he has to learn to live on his own. He cannot look to people for help.

Though it was hard, the volunteers gradually stopped spending so much time with Pearson. They fed him, but they did not pause to stroke his smooth gray fur, or to talk to him soothingly.

At first, Pearson seemed to miss his human companions. He watched for them. He scooted eagerly to the gate when they came to clean his pen or to bring him his dinner.

But gradually, he became more and more absorbed in his own affairs. He rested his head against the rim of the tank. He swam in circles, rippling the water with his flippers.

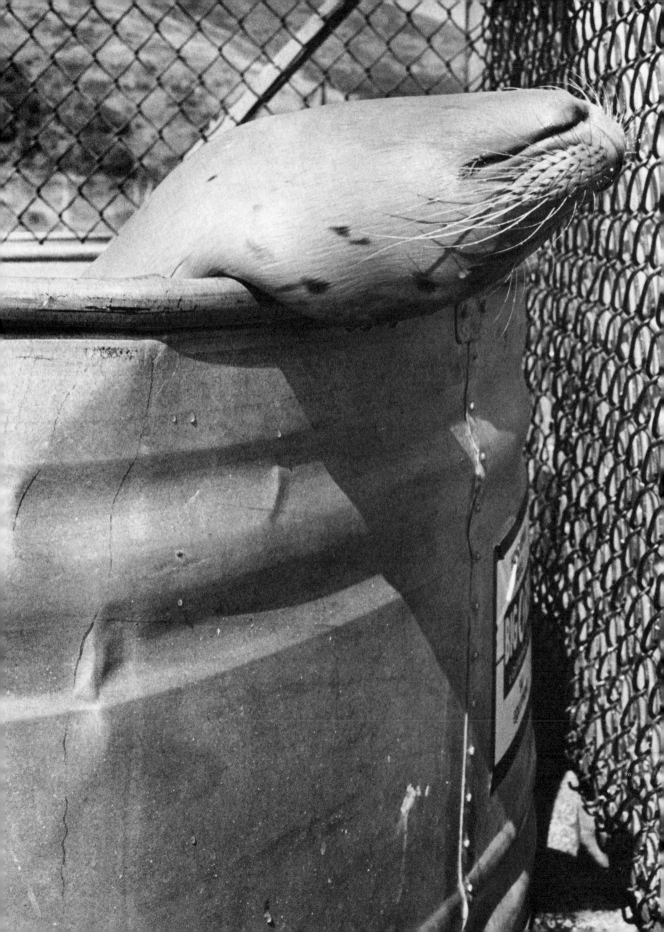

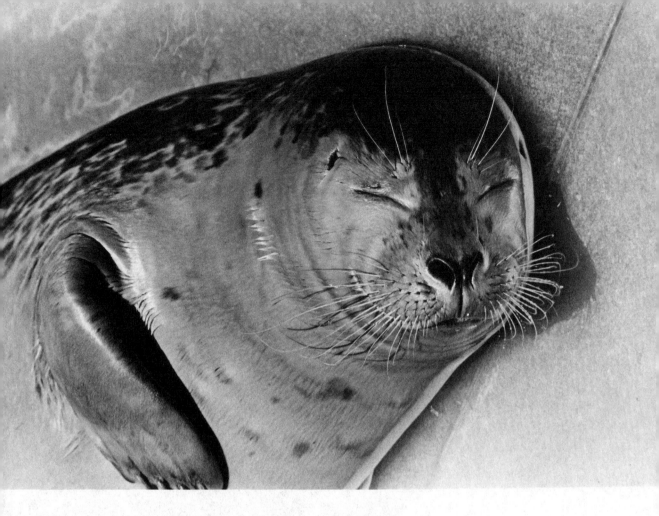

He slept in the warm summer sun.

He listened to sounds. The cry of a bird or the bark of a dog in the distance would make him lift up his head and open his earholes wide.

As the summer went on, Pearson's mind and body slowly changed. He no longer looked like a baby. He weighed more than 50 pounds. His shape was longer and sleeker. His head was slimmer. His coat was a darker shade of gray.

He was no longer very interested in his human keepers. Sometimes he growled when the person cleaning his pen came too near. One day when Holly tried to pick him up to weigh him, he gave her a bad nip on the chin.

These changes in personality were hard to take. But at the same time, the people who worked at the Center knew that they were necessary. They were succeeding in their task of making Pearson independent. Though he had lived almost his entire life in captivity, he was definitely not a pet. Now that his babyhood was over, his natural instincts as a wild animal were beginning to assert themselves. It would soon be time to send him home to the sea.

The release of an animal from the Marine Mammal Center is an important event. It has to be well planned. The time and the place must be chosen with care. And the animal must be ready, both physically and mentally.

Pearson was in excellent condition, and by late July he weighed more than 60 pounds. Though this was much less than the 300 to 350 pounds he would weigh when fully grown, it was still enough to protect him for the present. He was too big to be easy prey for the sharks and killer whales which hunted smaller seal pups. In addition, if he had difficulty finding food during his first days in the sea, his weight would sustain him until he became a skilled hunter.

But Holly wished that he were more familiar with his own kind.

Harbor seals are naturally sociable animals. When on land, they gather together in groups. Besides providing companionship, these groups give the seals a degree of safety which they would not have on their own. Within a group, danger is likely to be sensed more quickly. One seal can give warning, and all the seals can escape.

There was no doubt that Pearson would be safer if he could join a group of harbor seals. And it might be easier for him to do this if he had some companions of his own kind at the Center. But Holly could see no way of providing any.

Then one morning, two young harbor seals which had been found stranded on a beach were brought to the Center. They were somewhat smaller than Pearson and had respiratory infections. They would probably have died if they had not been rescued and treated with antibiotics. Within a few days, they began to recover. And very soon, Pearson had the company he needed.

Holly and the rest of the staff and volunteers had mixed feelings as they began to think about Pearson's release. On the one hand, they were proud of the work they had done in raising the young seal to be strong, healthy, and independent. But on the other hand, they would miss him.

It had become a habit, when arriving at work, to ask, "How's Pearson this morning?" Everyone liked to see him swimming round and round in his pool or basking in the warm sunshine. When he was gone, the Center wouldn't seem the same.

It wasn't easy, either, to decide where to let Pearson go. It would be simple to carry him down to the beach near the Center, but that was far from where he had been discovered as a young pup. Finally, a marshy area known as Mowry Slough was chosen. It was a two-hour drive from the Marine Mammal Center, but it was close to where Pearson had been found.

What was more, the Slough—which adjoins the San Francisco Bay—is part of a federal wildlife refuge. Visitors are not allowed to enter without special permission. Sharks are rarely seen in its waters. A group of harbor seals was already living there. Perhaps the very group to which Pearson's mother had belonged.

All in all, it was as safe and welcoming a place as could be found for Pearson to start his new life.

The day of the release—August 18—dawned cool and foggy. Pearson was alone in his tank. The other seals had been moved to another pen. They were not yet ready to be returned to the sea, and Holly wanted them out of the way as final arrangements for the release were made.

During the past week, Pearson had been fed an extra rich diet, including several buckets of live anchovies. Although live fish were too expensive to be fed to the seals on a regular basis, Holly wanted to be sure that he could cope with the kind of food he would have to eat in the sea. Fortunately, the anchovies were no problem for Pearson. Though he had never seen live food, he was able to catch and eat the swiftly moving fish with ease.

During the past week, Pearson had also begun to spend almost all his waking hours circling round and round his tank. A volunteer counted and found that he swam 600 circles in one hour.

Perhaps he was responding, in the only way he could, to some inner urge to travel. Or he may have been simply exercising. Whatever the explanation, there was no doubt that Pearson's activity was completely absorbing.

He hardly noticed when Holly entered the pen. And it was only when she reached into the tank and grabbed him by the rear flippers that he stopped swimming. He squirmed in protest as she hauled him out. And he puffed angrily as she attached a metal tag through the thin flesh of his rear flipper.

Holly and the volunteer holding Pearson down were sorry to have to hurt him, but the tag was very important. It had a number on it which would identify him if he were ever found on a beach. A tag was the only way the Center had of keeping track of an animal after it was released.

Next, Pearson was weighed one last time. Sixty-five pounds, the dial on the scale read. Holly and the volunteer holding him staggered under the load.

The rescue truck holding a metal carrying case had been backed up to the gate of the pen.

Holly grabbed Pearson by the tail. Then, with an effort, she swung him up and into the case. Quickly, the door was shut.

Pearson didn't know what was happening. He scratched frantically at the metal case. He pulled himself up by his front flippers and peered out the barred window.

Holly wished she could explain what was taking place. But she knew that Pearson wouldn't be able to understand. All she could say was: "Don't worry, fellow. It's going to be all right. You'll be swimming again soon. I promise."

The sun came out as the rescue truck traveled over the highway. When it arrived at the entrance to the wildlife refuge, reporters from a local newspaper and television station were waiting. People were interested in the work that was being done at the Marine Mammal Center. There had already been several news stories about Pearson. Now the camera and reporters wanted one last picture and one last word of farewell.

The woman who had found Pearson when he was a tiny pup was also there. She and a friend were studying the harbor seals living at Mowry Slough. They had brought sleeping bags so that they could spend the night in the marsh, watching Pearson and the other seals after the release.

An agent of the Fish and Wildlife Service, which manages the refuge, joined the group as they started over the bumpy dirt road which led to the Slough.

The marshes were filled with birds. Great flocks of avocets and phalaropes took to the sky as the truck moved slowly along the road.

At last it stopped. The case was lifted off. In the distance was an inlet of water. A group of harbor seals could be seen dozing on the far bank. But in between the road and the water lay the muddy marshland of Mowry Slough. The heavy case, with Pearson inside, would have to be carried through the marsh to the water's edge.

The moment Holly and the volunteers stepped into the tall grass, they knew that this was not going to be an easy release. Thick black mud sucked at their boots. Pearson shifted from side to side within the crate.

The mud became deeper and deeper. Finally, Holly decided that the weight of the case, together with Pearson, was just too much. A large piece of wet canvas had been put inside the case to keep Pearson cool during the journey. Now the door to the case was opened, and Pearson was quickly wrapped in the canvas. He would be carried the rest of the way in this makeshift sling.

The seals on the far bank of the inlet had taken to the water. Their round gray heads dotted the surface. They watched curiously as the strange procession made its way slowly toward them.

Suddenly Holly stumbled. In a second, she was floundering thigh-deep in mud. The canvas dropped. And all at once, Pearson was free. Everyone was confused. Some tried to help Holly. Others looked for Pearson. He seemed to have disappeared.

84-18

Then out of the reeds at the water's edge, his sleek gray form emerged.

"There he goes!" someone shouted.

Pearson was in the water. He was swimming. He was free. The heads of the harbor seals in the water bobbed down and then up again, watching.

Holly struggled for a footing on the slippery tufts of grass. She hadn't even seen Pearson slip away. Now all that could be glimpsed of him was a round gray head moving through the water.

For a moment, everyone fell silent. The months of patient care and tireless watching and waiting were over. Pearson was on his own.

There seemed to be only one thing to say. And Holly said it. "Good luck, Pearson," she shouted, as the sleek gray head suddenly disappeared beneath the water. "Good luck!"

ABOUT THE CALIFORNIA MARINE
MAMMAL CENTER

The California Marine Mammal Center was started in 1975 by Lloyd Smalley, a dedicated conservationist with a long-standing interest in marine mammals. It is located within the Golden Gate National Recreation Area in Marin County, California. The Center is staffed almost entirely by volunteers and is funded largely through private donations. The Marine Mammal Center performs three important functions.

First, it rescues and rehabilitates sick, injured, and abandoned marine mammals. Its rate of success in returning these animals to the sea is between 40 and 50 percent—an unusually high figure in the field of wildlife rescue and rehabilitation.

The Center also serves as a research facility. Veterinarians, animal behaviorists, and students of marine biology observe the activities of the seals and sea lions at the Center. They study the records which are kept on each animal. They perform autopsies on those that die.

Finally, the Center performs an important job of public education. Visitors are welcome. Groups of schoolchildren tour the Center, hear lectures, and see slide shows about marine mammals. The staff hopes that greater public knowledge about these animals will lead to greater public awareness of the steps which must be taken to protect and preserve their way of life in the sea.

INDEX